My Aunt
and the Animals

For Thirza and Rufus

First U.S. edition published in 1985 by Barron's Educational Series, Inc.

Text © Elizabeth MacDonald 1985
Illustrations © Annie Owen 1985

This book has been designed and produced by
Aurum Press Ltd., 33 Museum Street,
London WC1A 1LD, England.

All inquiries should be addressed to:
Barron's Educational Series, Inc.
113 Crossways Park Drive
Woodbury, New York 11797

International Standard Book No. 0-8120-5641-8
Library of Congress Catalog Card No.

PRINTED IN BELGIUM
5 6 7 8   9 8 7 6 5 4 3 2 1

My Aunt
and the Animals

by Elizabeth MacDonald and Annie Owen

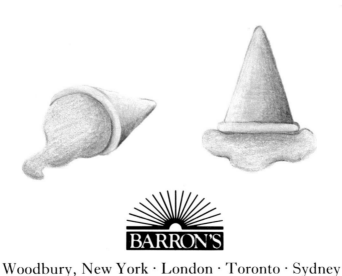

BARRON'S

Woodbury, New York · London · Toronto · Sydney

My aunt has always enjoyed being with animals . . .

In the month of January, my aunt went to a play
and sat behind an enormous elephant
eating an extra-large ice-cream.

In the month of February, my aunt went skating
and bumped into two stripy tigers trying to tango.
    Two stripy tigers
    – and one enormous elephant eating two large ice-creams.

In the month of March, my aunt went to a fair
and saw three brown bears blowing up balloons.
Three brown bears,
Two stripy tigers
– and one enormous elephant eating three large ice-creams.

In the month of April, my aunt went on a picnic
and came across four feathery flamingos fishing for frogs.
Four feathery flamingos,
Three brown bears,
Two stripy tigers
– and one enormous elephant eating four large ice-creams.

In the month of May, when my aunt went to a concert,
she watched five prickly porcupines playing the piano.
    Five prickly porcupines,
    Four feathery flamingos,
    Three brown bears,
    Two stripy tigers
    – and one enormous elephant eating five large ice-creams.

In the month of June, my aunt went to the circus
where six cheerful chimpanzees were chasing after clowns.
    Six cheerful chimpanzees,
    Five prickly porcupines,
    Four feathery flamingos,
    Three brown bears,
    Two stripy tigers
    – and one enormous elephant eating six large ice-creams.

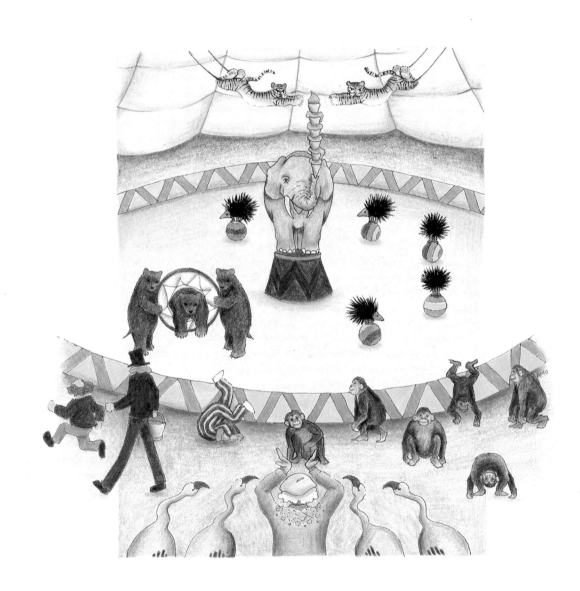

In the month of July, my aunt went to the seaside
and joined seven silly sea-lions skipping on the sand.
    Seven silly sea-lions,
    Six cheerful chimpanzees,
    Five prickly porcupines,
    Four feathery flamingos,
    Three brown bears,
    Two stripy tigers
    – and one enormous elephant eating seven large ice-creams.

In the month of August, when my aunt went to the races,
eight crazy kangaroos collided on the course.
  Eight crazy kangaroos,
  Seven silly sea-lions,
  Six cheerful chimpanzees,
  Five prickly porcupines,
  Four feathery flamingos,
  Three brown bears,
  Two stripy tigers
  – and one enormous elephant eating eight large ice-creams.

In the month of September, my aunt went boating
and passed nine rare rhinoceroses rowing on the river.
    Nine rare rhinoceroses,
    Eight crazy kangaroos,
    Seven silly sea-lions,
    Six cheerful chimpanzees,
    Five prickly porcupines,
    Four feathery flamingos,
    Three brown bears,
    Two stripy tigers
    – and one enormous elephant eating nine large ice-creams.

In the month of October, my aunt went to the bank
and found ten crotchety toucans queueing up for cash.
   Ten crotchety toucans,
   Nine rare rhinoceroses,
   Eight crazy kangaroos,
   Seven silly sea-lions,
   Six cheerful chimpanzees,
   Five prickly porcupines,
   Four feathery flamingos,
   Three brown bears,
   Two stripy tigers
   – and one enormous elephant eating ten large ice-creams.

In the month of November, my aunt went Christmas shopping.
Eleven eager alligators were gift-wrapping gloves.

Eleven eager alligators,
Ten crotchety toucans,
Nine rare rhinoceroses,
Eight crazy kangaroos,
Seven silly sea-lions,
Six cheerful chimpanzees,
Five prickly porcupines,
Four feathery flamingos,
Three brown bears,
Two stripy tigers
– and one enormous elephant eating eleven large ice-creams.

In the month of December, my aunt threw a party.
She invited twelve tired tortoises to try out the treats.
Twelve tired tortoises,
Eleven eager alligators,
Ten crotchety toucans,
Nine rare rhinoceroses,
Eight crazy kangaroos,
Seven silly sea-lions,
Six cheerful chimpanzees,
Five prickly porcupines,
Four feathery flamingos,
Three brown bears,
Two stripy tigers . . .

– and one *enormous* elephant (to help eat up the ice-cream)
all came to my aunt's party to share the Christmas cheer!